JORDAN AND ALL THE FAVOURITES

By Emily Goldsmith

Illustrated by Susie Wilson

Emily Goldsmith
Jordan And All The Favourites ISBN-10: 197447092X ISBN-13: 9781974470921
Published in French as Les endroits préférés de Maxim
Copyright © 2017 Emily Goldsmith
All rights reserved under International and Pan-American Copyright Conventions.
Manufactured in the United States of America
Editor: Lori Bamber
Illustrator: Susie Wilson
Publishing Support: The Self Publishing Agency

For more information visit www.emilygoldsmith.ca.

For you, and all your favourites.

At lunch on Monday, Jordan and their friends sat down to eat beside the basketball court. Jordan was excited.

"This is my favourite place to eat lunch!" they said to their friends Olivia, Sam and Alex. "It's my favourite because when I finish, I can play basketball."

Their friends all smiled. "This is a great place to eat, Jordan," said Olivia.

The four friends talked and ate, and when they had all finished their lunches, they went to play basketball.

5

At lunch on Tuesday, Jordan and their friends sat down to eat by the soccer field. "This is my favourite place to eat lunch," Jordan said happily. "It's my favourite because when I finish, I can play soccer."

Olivia frowned. "It is a great place to eat, Jordan. But yesterday you said that the basketball court is your favourite – you *can't* have two favourites."

6

Jordan put down their sandwich. "Oh," they said, confused.

After they had all finished their lunches, the four friends ran to play soccer.

At lunch on Wednesday, Jordan and their friends sat down to eat by the playground.

"This is my favourite place to eat lunch," Jordan said. "It's my favourite because when I finish, I can play on the swings and stuff."

Sam frowned. "It is a great place to eat, Jordan. But yesterday, you said that the soccer field is your favourite, and on Monday, you said that the basketball court is your favourite. You *can't* have three favourites," she said.

"Oh," said Jordan.

The four friends finished eating their lunches and then ran to play on the playground. But somehow, it just didn't feel as fun as usual.

At lunch on Thursday, Jordan and their friends sat down to eat on the carpet in the classroom.

"This is my favourite place to eat lunch," Jordan said. "It's my favourite because when I finish, I can play board games."

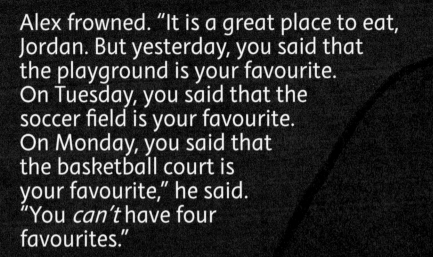

Alex frowned. "It is a great place to eat, Jordan. But yesterday, you said that the playground is your favourite. On Tuesday, you said that the soccer field is your favourite. On Monday, you said that the basketball court is your favourite," he said. "You *can't* have four favourites."

Jordan said nothing.

The four friends finished eating their lunches and then quietly played board games together.

At lunch on Friday, Jordan and their friends sat down to eat near the hopscotch court.

"This is my favourite place to eat lunch," Jordan thought. "It's my favourite because when I finish, I can play hopscotch."

Even though Jordan loved playing hopscotch, and had their favourite sandwich — cucumber and cream cheese — they felt a bit sad.

"You don't seem like yourself today, Jordan," said Ms. Chin, the lunch supervisor. "Is there something wrong?"

"I don't know," said Jordan. "My friends say that I can't have more than one favourite place to eat my lunch. But that can't be true, because I have lots of favourites."

"Oh, dear," Ms. Chin replied, putting a hand on Jordan's shoulder. She was quiet for a minute. "How about you go and talk to Mr. Brar about this? I think he will be able to help you."

"Okay," Jordan said. "Thank you."

They picked up their sandwich, put it back in their lunch bag, and went to see Mr. Brar in his office.

"Mr. Brar?" Jordan said quietly, knocking on the open door. "Can I come in?"

"Of course, Jordan," said Mr. Brar with a big smile. "So nice to see you!"

Jordan looked down at their shoelaces. They could feel tears starting to sting their eyes.

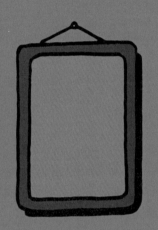

Concerned, Mr. Brar asked, "What's going on, Jordan?"

Jordan started to cry.

"On Monday, I ate my lunch beside the basketball court, and that's my favourite place to eat because when I finish, I can play basketball.

On Tuesday, I ate my lunch by the soccer field, and that's my favourite place to eat because when I finish, I can play soccer.

On Wednesday, I ate my lunch at the playground, and that's my favourite place to eat because when I finish, I can play on the swings and stuff.

16

Yesterday, I ate my lunch on the carpet in the classroom, and that's my favourite place to eat because when I finish, I can play board games.

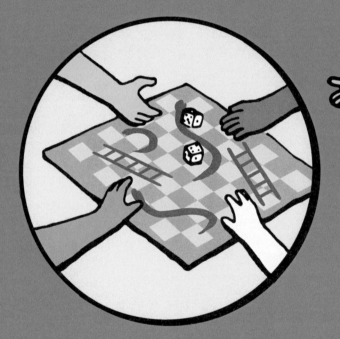

But my friends say I *can't* have more than one favourite," they finished, taking a deep breath.

"But I can't help it! Those are all my favourites. And I have more favourites, too."

Mr. Brar smiled.

"I understand," he said kindly. "I have to go and meet my partner for lunch at our favourite restaurant, Leo's. But I'd love to talk more about this with you later." He got up from his chair.

"Leo's?" Jordan asked. They didn't know that restaurant.

"Yep," said Mr. Brar. "We love Leo's. We go there a lot. It's our favourite because they have a pasta special."

Jordan was curious. "But what if you wanted to go somewhere else?"

"Well, we do," Mr. Brar said. "Our other favourite is eating at home. It's our favourite because we can eat in our pyjamas."

Jordan sat up straighter. "What if you wanted to eat at the basketball court? Could you do that if it was your favourite?"

"Yes, we could eat at the basketball court. It could be our favourite, too," Mr. Brar said.

"How about at the soccer field, if that was your favourite?" Jordan was excited.

"Yes, we could eat at the soccer field. It could be our favourite, too," Mr. Brar said.

"And the playground? Or the classroom?" Jordan asked. They were smiling now, too.

"Of course we could eat by the playground or in the classroom," Mr. Brar said. "Having more than one favourite means that you have so much happiness and love in your heart, it couldn't possibly all be for just one favourite."

"Thank you, Mr. Brar!" Jordan jumped up out of their seat. "I'm going to go finish my sandwich now!"

They gave him a high-five, then raced out of the office and back to the four-square court.

"Hi, Jordan!" said Olivia.

"Hi, Olivia," said Jordan as they sat down and took out their sandwich again.

"This is my favourite place to eat lunch," Jordan said, with a big smile on their face. "It's my favourite because when I'm finished, I can play hopscotch."

Olivia frowned. "Yesterday, you said –"

"Olivia, people *can* have more than one favourite," said Jordan, stopping her. "I have lots of favourites because I have too much happiness and love in my heart for just one."

"Oh," Olivia said, surprised. "I didn't think of it that way."

"Me neither," Sam said thoughtfully.

"You're pretty lucky to have so much love and happiness in your heart, Jordan," said Alex.

Jordan just smiled, finished their sandwich, and then went to play hopscotch with their friends.

On Monday, Jordan grabbed their
lunch and headed for the door
as soon as the bell rang. On their
way out, they saw Mr. Brar.

"Hi, Mr. Brar!" said Jordan
cheerfully.

"Where are you going to eat
today, Jordan?" asked Mr. Brar
with a smile.

Jordan smiled back. "Oh, that's
easy," they replied.

26

"At my favourite place!"

Emily Goldsmith is a queer teacher living in the Greater Vancouver area. She is a Sexual Orientation & Gender Identity (SOGI) Lead at the elementary school where she teaches, and previously volunteered with Out On Campus at Simon Fraser University. She has degrees in French and Education from SFU. Emily hopes that her writing can help children find the bravery to be who they are. Some of Emily's favourite things are books, puzzles, running, and ice cream. Learn more at emilygoldsmith.ca

Susie Wilson is a queer cisgender woman. She is an illustrator and comic artist currently living in Vancouver, where she is studying for her BFA in Fine Arts at Emily Carr University. She hopes to use her art to help young LGBT people feel recognized and represented. Find her on social media @mazarbor

Photo by Meesha Raczova (ratzlaffphoto.com)

Made in the USA
San Bernardino, CA
17 September 2017